18   2^{00}
child

DOGGIE DUTIES

Jamie Michalak

CANDLEWICK
ENTERTAINMENT

Major funding for *Fetch!* is provided by the National Science Foundation and public television viewers.
This *Fetch!* material is based upon work supported by the National Science Foundation
under Grant No. 0813513. Any opinions, findings, and conclusions
or recommendations expressed in this material are those of the author(s)
and do not necessarily reflect the views of the National Science Foundation.

First edition 2014

Library of Congress Catalog Card Number 2012950641
ISBN 978-0-7636-7277-5 (hardcover)
ISBN 978-0-7636-6815-0 (paperback)

13 14 15 16 17 18 SWT 10 9 8 7 6 5 4 3 2 1

Printed in Dongguan, Guangdong, China

This book was typeset in Adobe Caslon Semibold.
The illustrations were created digitally.

Candlewick Entertainment
An imprint of Candlewick Press
99 Dover Street
Somerville, Massachusetts 02144

visit us at www.candlewick.com

CONTENTS

CHAPTER ONE
The Golden Blobby

It all started when Ruff Ruffman, host of the game show *FETCH!*, found out that he had won a major award.

And it ended with Ruff stuck in a mouse hole. But it's a long story, so let's start at the beginning.

Early one morning, the phone rang.

"Oh, happy day! I won a Golden Blobby!" Ruff

yelled to Blossom, his trusty show supervisor,

after he hung up the phone. Blossom just

scratched her head.

"You don't know what a Golden Blobby is?" he asked. She shook her head. "It's only the biggest award in the dog world!"

That afternoon the award was delivered.

"*Oof!*" Ruff said, lugging it inside. "It might also be the heaviest award in the dog world."

That's when Ruff's mouse assistant, Chet, scurried out of his mouse hole.

Chet, who is quite strong for a mouse, picked the Golden Blobby up and set it on Blossom's desk.

Blossom did not look pleased.

"I got it for the luge-race episode," Ruff told Chet. "Remember that one? This definitely makes up for finishing last."

Blossom pointed to the bathroom door.

"You think we should keep it in the
bathroom?" Ruff asked. Blossom nodded.
"Fine. I have to use the bathroom anyway,"
Ruff said. "I'll put it on the shelf above
the toilet."

Ruff took the Blobby and went to the bathroom.

A moment later, there was a *bang!* And a *crash!* And a *squeak!*

Ruff ran out of the bathroom.

"THE BLOBBY BROKE THE
TOILET!" he shouted.

Blossom dialed the plumber. But his
message said he was on vacation until
next week.

"Oh, no! I really have to go," Ruff cried.

Blossom offered her litter box, but Ruff refused it. "When a dog uses a litter box, he's no longer a dog," he said. "I need a toilet that doesn't break. NASA should be working on this!"

Blossom showed Ruff on the computer that NASA *does* work on toilets.

"NASA's in the plumbing business now?" Ruff said. "Guess things have really gone down the toilet over there."

Then Blossom pointed out that though NASA makes *space* toilets, only astronauts get to use them.

"No problem," Ruff said. "I'll train to be an astronaut so I can use one of those NASA toilets. I'm a whiz at space stuff. Oh, why did I have to say 'whiz'?"

CHAPTER TWO
Water, Water Everywhere

"Welcome to Space Camp," Ruff said.

"I need to prepare to go into the unknown . . . on a mission to get a toilet!"

Training wouldn't be easy, but Ruff was up for a challenge. Also, he had no choice!

Ruff even had a flight suit he'd picked up at a flea market a few years ago, just in case he ever needed it. He had some trouble getting it to zip up, though.

After some rigorous exercise, he managed
to get it on — mostly.

"Never mind," said Ruff. "In space, I won't weigh anything anyway, right? That means I can still eat Chinese food!"

Blossom didn't look impressed, but she nodded.

She showed Ruff that astronauts eat the same foods we do here. But lots of it is freeze-dried. That means that the water has been taken out, so the food lasts longer and is easier to pack. When you're ready to eat, you just add water and—voilà!—fried rice.

YUM

Speaking of water, what was Chet doing?

"Chet!" Ruff yelled. "Please don't water that cactus right now! I mean, really!"

The last thing Ruff wanted to think about was water!

Then Blossom showed Ruff that to get clean, astronauts spray themselves with water. Then they use a vacuum hose to suck the water off their skin.

That's when they heard running water.

"Chet!" Ruff cried. "Do you have to take a

shower in the sink *right now*? Seriously!"

"OK," Ruff continued. "Now give me the poop—I mean, *scoop*—on space toilets." Blossom showed Ruff her notes on the NASA space toilet.

"So, space toilets are like the ones we have here on Earth," Ruff said.

"But they use air instead of water to move waste?"

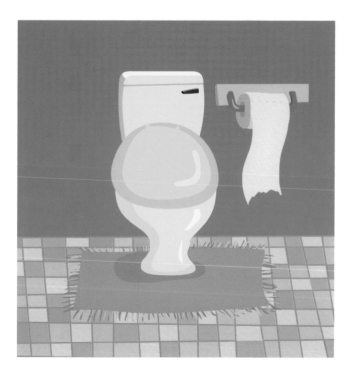

Blossom nodded, then showed Ruff her
computer again.

"Wow, looks
like we can make
our *own* space toilet.
Well, what are
we waiting for?
Let's get started!"

But Ruff was interrupted again.

"CHET!" he hollered. "MUST YOU INSTALL A ROMAN FOUNTAIN IN MY DOGHOUSE RIGHT NOW?"

CHAPTER THREE
How to Make a Space Toilet

Houston, we have a problem. It turns out that Blossom's space toilet wasn't exactly what Ruff had in mind.

"Are you kidding?" he cried. "On the International Space Station, urine is recycled into drinking water? *Ewww!*"

Blossom showed Ruff that NASA recycles its water to make room for other stuff on board the ship. Astronauts pee into a sort of vacuum cleaner hose, and the urine is filtered, then returned to the cabin. It ends up cleaner than bottled water.

"I hate vacuum cleaners!" Ruff said. "I'd rather use the litter box. And you know how I feel about dogs using litter boxes."

But Blossom was already getting rocks and sand—and pasta!—to make a filter.

"Are you filtering pee or making dinner?" Ruff asked. "I guess uncooked pasta could trap some of the particles. And even I know that rocks and sand filter rain in Earth's water cycle, but I'm still not sure I want to drink pee water!"

Then Blossom started to pour some dirty water through the filter, to show Ruff how it worked.

That's when Ruff yelled, "I can't hold it anymore! Call NASA and get me one of their pee-recycling vacuum toilets. I don't care if I'm afraid of vacuums. I'll use it!"

Blossom went back to NASA's website to order a toilet. She gasped, then shook her head.

"What?" Ruff asked. "What do you mean, the only vacuum toilet left is on the shuttle that's launching *right now*?"

3 ... 2 ... 1 ...

They watched the shuttle blast off on the

screen.

"NOOOOOOOOO!" Ruff shouted. "My toilet! Come back!"

Ruff sighed. "Well, isn't that always the way?" he asked. "You finally find a NASA vacuum toilet, and it winds up in space!"

Suddenly, he noticed Chet's mouse hole.

"Hmm. He must have a bathroom in there," Ruff said. He peered inside.

"Whoa. Nice digs! So peaceful, so calm—so clean! Who knew Chet was such a stylish guy? He even has one of those composting toilets! But it's too small for me. Waaay too small . . . I think," Ruff said, trying to squeeze into the mouse hole.

There was no way he could fit.

Ruff tried to pull his head back out.

But it was stuck.

"Blossom! Chet!" he cried. "Get me
out of here!"

And *that's* how Ruff ended up stuck in a mouse hole.

"Argh!" Ruff cried. "Nature is calling, but I can't answer! Oh, where's a fire hydrant when you need one?

"Don't worry," Ruff said. "I'm sure I'll find a way out of this tight spot. See you next time — hopefully things will be bladder . . . er, better! In the meantime, Blossom, can you bring me your litter box?"

SCIENCE ACTIVITY
Blossom's Water Filter

Can you help Ruff out and learn how to clean dirty water using Blossom's instructions?

WHAT YOU'LL NEED:

a 2-liter soda bottle cut in half (by an adult)

water

a bowl

FILTER MATERIALS: a coffee filter, napkins, or paper towels, activated carbon (sold at aquarium shops), gravel, sand, crushed stone, and uncooked macaroni

WATER CONTAMINANTS: salt, dirt, grass, cooking oil, food coloring, beans, and/or tiny pieces of paper

This book belongs to

....

No
Wolves

This is the story of three little pigs,

and houses built of straw, bricks, twigs.

There's something else.

Can you guess what?

On every page there's a pot to spot!

Three Little Pigs

Nick and Claire Page

Illustrations by Katie Saunders

make
believe
ideas

Three little pigs left home one day,
packed their bags and went on their way.
Mother Pig said, "Good bye, bye, bye!"
But a wolf saw them go and thought,
"Mmm – PORK PIE!"

Blue Prints

Houses from Straw

The first little pig met a man selling straw.
"Will it make a good house? I'm not quite sure."
So he paid for the bales and stacked them high,
but the wolf licked his lips, thinking,
"Mmm — STIR FRY!"

The second little pig met a man selling wood.
"I think I'll build with this, it looks quite good.
So he worked all day and did not stop,
but the wolf licked his lips, thinking,
"Mmm — PORK CHOP!"

25% off

Edward
Woodwood
Supplies

11

The third little pig met a man selling bricks.
"These look strong, much better than sticks."
So he built his house, all shiny and new,
but the wolf licked his lips, thinking,
"Mmm — BARBECUE!"

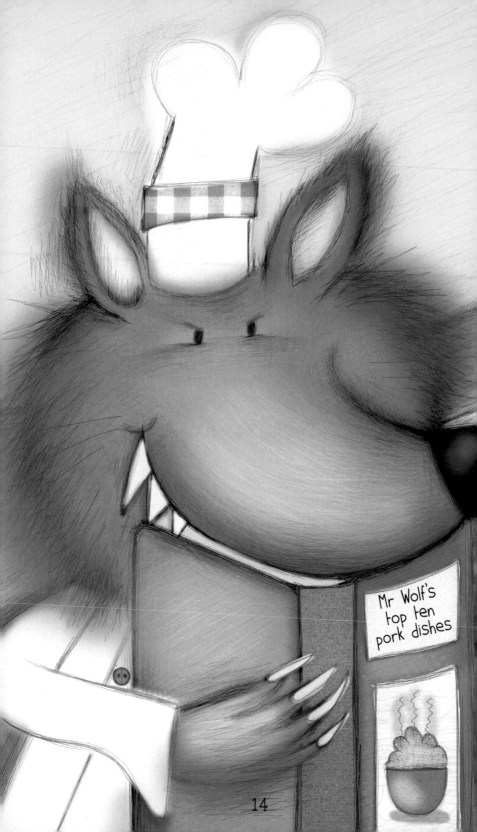

Mr Wolf's
top ten
pork dishes

14

When the homes were finished
by the piggies three,
they went inside to cook their tea.
But the wolf was feeling very hungry too,
and the wolf licked his lips, thinking,
"Mmm — PORK STEW!"

16

Said the wolf to Piggy Straw, "Now let me in!"
"Not by the hair on my chinny chin chin!"
So the wolf huffed and puffed,
and the house went WHAM!
And the wolf licked his lips, shouting,
"Mmm — BOILED HAM!"

17

Piggy Straw ran straight
to the house of Piggy Wood.
And behind him came the wolf,
"Let me in! I'll be good!"

Then he huffed and he puffed,
and the house went SMASH!
And the wolf licked his lips, shouting,
"Mmm — GOULASH!"

Then the two pigs ran
to the house made of bricks.
They were chased by the wolf
(who was not quite as quick).
There he huffed and he puffed,
but the house stayed whole.
So, the wolf climbed the roof, shouting,
"Mmm — CASSEROLE!"

No Salesmen
No Wolves
Please!

Then the three pigs ran
and they fetched a pot.
"Quick, quick," said Piggy Bricks,
"let's make it hot!"
As the hungry wolf jumped
down the chimney tower,
he landed in the pot and screamed,
"Oww — SWEET AND SOUR!"

23

He jumped out quick and ran far away
from the bricks, the wood and the pile of hay.

And the lesson of this story is —
learn it quick —
don't be a silly sausage —
make your house out of bricks!

Ready to tell

Oh no! Some of the pictures from this story have been mixed up! Can you retell the story and point to each picture in the correct order?

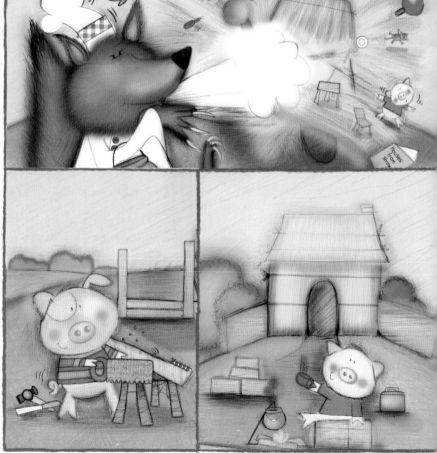

Picture dictionary

Encourage your child to read these words from the story and gradually develop his or her basic vocabulary.

bricks

builds

chimney

climbs

house

pot

straw

wolf

wood

Key words

Here are some key words used in context. Help
your child to use other words from the border
in simple sentences.

The three little pigs
pack their bags.

The pig builds a
house out **of** wood.

"I will blow your house
down!" says Mr Wolf.

Mr Wolf falls into
a pot of hot water.

Mr Wolf runs **away**.

Build a house

The three little pigs were good at building houses. Now it's your turn to have a go — here's how!

You will need

3 small cardboard boxes • scissors • glue • marker pen • paper • card • straw • twigs • paint • sponge

What to do

1 Cover each box with paper and glue it on.
2 Use the marker pen to draw a door and windows. Ask a grown-up to help you cut them out.
3 Glue the straw or twigs onto the sides of two of the boxes. For the brick house, cut a small rectangle of sponge and apply paint. Then stamp rows of bricks on the walls.
4 To make the roof, cut out a rectangle of card and fold it down the middle. Glue on your chosen covering. Put glue on the top edges of your box and carefully stick down the roof.

Hints and tips

• If you don't have straw, try using packing material, raffia, yellow tissue, or crêpe paper twisted into strips.
• Use ice-lolly sticks or toothpicks instead of twigs.
• Make a garden, with trees made from pine cones and pigs made from corks!